For Jack, Anna, and Natalie
—MM

For Tom and Charlie Mumford
and for Siwan
—AA

First American edition published in 2007 by Carolrhoda Books, Inc.

Text © 2006 by Margaret Mayo
Illustrations © 2006 by Alex Ayliffe

Originally published in 2006 by Orchard Books, London, England

Carolrhoda Books, Inc.
A division of Lerner Publishing Group
241 First Avenue North
Minneapolis, MN 55401 U.S.A.

Website address: www.lernerbooks.com

rary of Congress Cataloging-in-Publication Data

1935–

t Mayo ; illustrated by Alex Ayliffe. — 1st American ed.

England : Orchard Books, 2006.
(lib. bdg. : alk. paper)
rature. I. Ayliffe, Alex, ill. II. Title.

2006029853

Margaret Mayo & Alex Ayliffe

ROAR!

CAROLRHODA BOOKS, INC. MINNEAPOLIS · NEW YORK

Bold **lions** love roar, **roar**, **roaring**,
while cubs play—racing, chasing,
scrambling over lionesses and—oops!—tumbling.
So **roar**, bold lions, **roar!**

Wrinkly **elephants** love **mud-wallowing**, squishy-squashy! Squishy-squashy! Squelching, trunks sucking and—shwoo-**oosh!**—water squirting. So **wallow**, wrinkly elephants, **wallow!**

Stripy **zebras** love **fast galloping,**
dumm-dd-dum! Hooves drumming,

manes rippling, tails flying.
So gallop, stripy zebras, gallop!

Fierce **tigers** love prowl, **prowl, prowling,**
through the jungle slowly s l i n k i n g,

softly creeping, no . . . grr . . . growling.
So **prowl**, fierce tigers, **prowl!**

Tall **giraffes** love stretch, stretch, stretching, long necks going up...up...reaching,

Black tongues flicking, lips leaf picking.
So stretch, tall giraffes, stretch!

Spunky **monkeys** love swing, swing, **swinging,**
hanging, dangling, tightly clinging,

treetop scampering, calling and screaming.

So swing, spunky monkeys, **swing!**

Plump **hippos** love swim, swim, **swimming**, floating, underwater strolling, and opening their giant mouths . . . **waaaahh** . . . till all their teeth are showing.

So swim, plump hippos, **swim!**

Spotty **leopards** love climb, **climb**, **climbing**,
up tree trunks zipping, sharp claws gripping,
among the green leaves, crouching, hiding.
So **climb**, spotty leopards, **climb**!

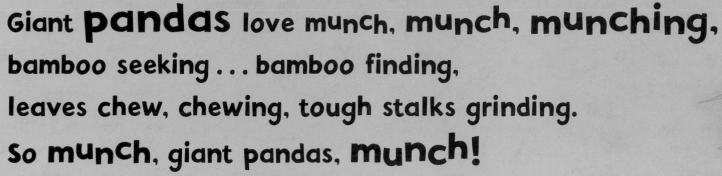

Giant **pandas** love munch, **munch**, **munching**,
bamboo seeking ... bamboo finding,
leaves chew, chewing, tough stalks grinding.
So **munch**, giant pandas, **munch!**

Bouncy **kangaroos** love jump, jump, jumping,
hopping, bounding, and . . . bumpety–bumping!
Little joey in the pouch, eyes peeping.
So **jump**, bouncy kangaroos, **jump!**

Grizzly **bears** love **fish, fish, fishing,**
in fast rivers *splishing, splashing,*

paws catching, jaws quickly snatching.
So fish, grizzly bears, **fish!**

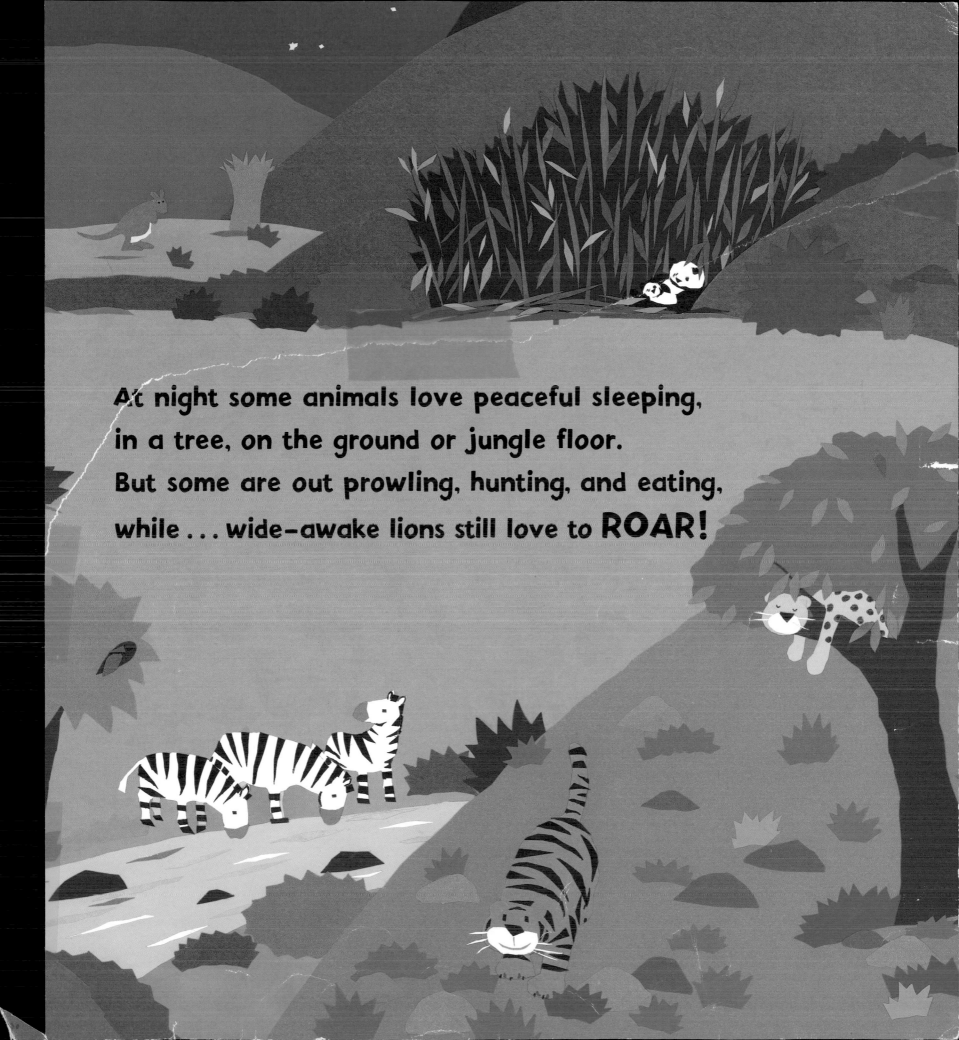

At night some animals love peaceful sleeping,
in a tree, on the ground or jungle floor.
But some are out prowling, hunting, and eating,
while . . . wide-awake lions still love to **ROAR!**